Joey the Juggler

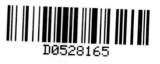

First published in 2008
by Wayland

Text copyright © Penny Dolan 2008
Illustration copyright © Bruno Robert 2008

Wayland
338 Euston Road
London NW1 3BH

Wayland Australia
Level 17/207 Kent Street
Sydney, NSW 2000

The rights of Penny Dolan to be identified as the Author and
Bruno Robert to be identified as the Illustrator of this Work have been
asserted by them in accordance with the Copyright, Designs and Patents Act, 1988.

All rights reserved

Series Editor: Louise John
Editor: Katie Powell
Cover design: Paul Cherrill
Design: D.R.ink
Consultant: Shirley Bickler

A CIP catalogue record for this book is available from the British Library.

ISBN 9781526302458

Printed in China

FSC
www.fsc.org
MIX
Paper from
responsible sources
FSC® C104740

Wayland is a division of Hachette Children's Books,
an Hachette UK Company

www.hachette.co.uk

Joey the Juggler

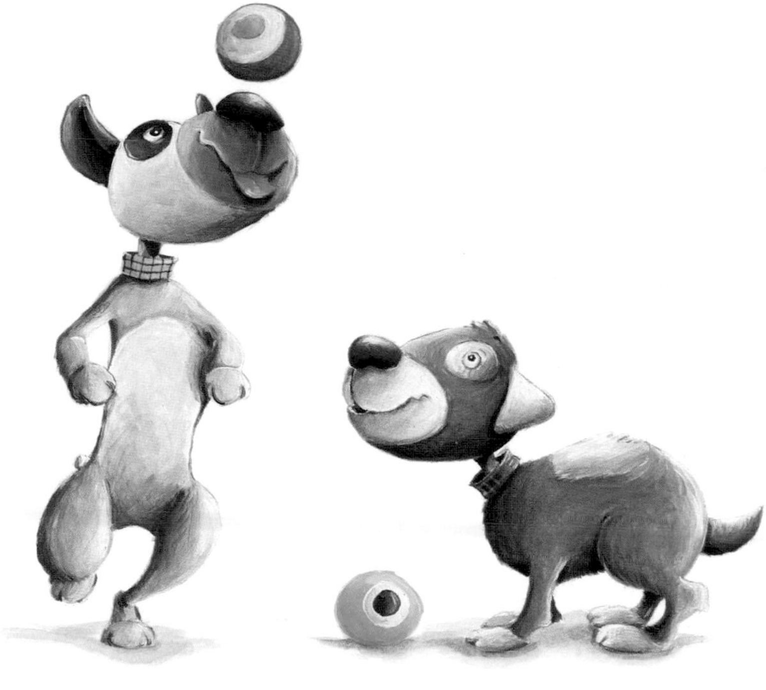

Written by Penny Dolan
Illustrated by Bruno Robert

WAYLAND

Joey was the juggler in
Carlo's Circus.

He had a very small caravan.

So Joey had to try out his tricks outside.

Up went the balls and down came the balls.

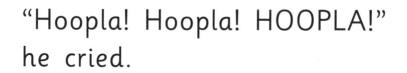

"Hoopla! Hoopla! HOOPLA!" he cried.

Up went the sticks and down came the sticks.

"Hoopla! Hoopla! HOOPLA!"

Up went the hoops and down came the hoops.

"Hoopla! Hoopla! HOOPLA!"
he cried.

“There is too much noise!” shouted Madam Crystal. “Too much HOOPLA! Go somewhere else!”

But Joey had nowhere else to do his juggling.

He had to try out his
tricks outside!

Madam Crystal was coming back from the shops.

She wanted to make some pancakes.

Yap and Scrap, the circus dogs, raced and chased around her.

They raced in front of her feet.

Oops! Up went Madam Crystal's box of eggs...

...and down came
those eggs.

1, 2, 3, 4, 5, 6, 7, 8, 9, 10!

Joey caught every one of them.

"Hoopla! Hoopla! HOOPLA!" he cried.

Madam Crystal laughed.
"Thank you, Joey. You can juggle here anytime!"

START READING is a series of highly enjoyable books for beginner readers. **The books have been carefully graded to match the Book Bands widely used in schools.** This enables readers to be sure they choose books that match their own reading ability.

Look out for the Band colour on the book in our Start Reading logo.

The Bands are:

Pink Band 1

Red Band 2

Yellow Band 3

Blue Band 4

Green Band 5

Orange Band 6

Turquoise Band 7

Purple Band 8

Gold Band 9

START READING books can be read independently or shared with an adult. They promote the enjoyment of reading through satisfying stories supported by fun illustrations.

Penny Dolan had great fun writing about Carlo's Circus, because she could pretend she was an expert juggler, brave trapeze artist, cheeky clown and an amazing elephant rider – even though she's definitely not!

Bruno Robert lives and works in Normandy, France, where he was born. He always wanted to draw and play with colours. When he is illustrating a story like this one, he likes to think of a bright and colourful world that is full of humour.